Looking at Animal Parts

Let's Look at Animal Bottoms

by Wendy Perkins

Consulting Editor: Gail Saunders-Smith, PhD

Consultant: Suzanne B. McLaren, Collections Manager
Section of Mammals, Carnegie Museum of Natural History
Edward O'Neil Research Center, Pittsburgh, Pennsylvania

Capstone press

Mankato, Minnesota

Pebble Plus is published by Capstone Press,
151 Good Counsel Drive, P.O. Box 669, Mankato, Minnesota 56002.
www.capstonepress.com

1 2 3 4 5 6 12 11 10 09 08 07

Library of Congress Cataloging-in-Publication Data
Perkins, Wendy, 1957–
    Let's look at animal bottoms / by Wendy Perkins.
    p. cm.—(Pebble plus. Looking at animal parts)
    Summary: "Simple text and photographs present a variety of animal bottoms and their uses"—Provided
by publisher.
    Includes bibliographical references and index.
    ISBN-13: 978-0-7368-6715-3 (hardcover)
    ISBN-10: 0-7368-6715-5 (hardcover)
    1. Buttocks—Juvenile literature. I. Title. II. Series.
QL950.39.P47 2007
571.3'1—dc22   2006020934

Editorial Credits
Sarah L. Schuette, editor; Kia Adams, set designer; Renée Doyle, book designer; Charlene Deyle, photo
    researcher; Scott Thoms, photo editor

Photo Credits
Corbis/Jeffrey L. Rotman, 16–17; Gallo Images/Martin Harvey, 11
Dwight R. Kuhn, 13
Getty Images Inc./Stone/Paul Souders, cover
James P. Rowan, 18–19
Lynn M. Stone, 15
McDonald Wildlife Photography/Joe McDonald, 4–5; Mary Ann McDonald, 1
Shutterstock/Geoffrey Kuchera, 9; Holly Kuchera, 6–7
SuperStock/age fotostock, 20–21

Note to Parents and Teachers

The Looking at Animal Parts set supports national science standards related to life
science. This book describes and illustrates animal bottoms. The images support
early readers in understanding the text. The repetition of words and phrases helps early
readers learn new words. This book also introduces early readers to subject-specific
vocabulary words, which are defined in the Glossary section. Early readers may need
assistance to read some words and to use the Table of Contents, Glossary, Read More,
Internet Sites, and Index sections of the book.

Table of Contents

Bottoms at Work

Animals sit on their bottoms.
Animals use their bottoms
to protect themselves
or to send messages.

A curious bear cub
walks up to a skunk.
The skunk gets scared
and turns around.

The skunk sprays a stinky
liquid from its bottom.
The cub runs away.

Kinds of Bottoms

Koalas have soft bottoms.

Koalas use their bottoms

to help them stay in trees.

Bees have sharp stingers
on their bottoms.
The stinger comes off
when a bee uses it.

Chickens sit down

to lay eggs.

They squeeze and squeeze.

Eggs come out

of their bottoms.

Sea cucumbers shoot sticky
threads out of their bottoms
when they are scared.

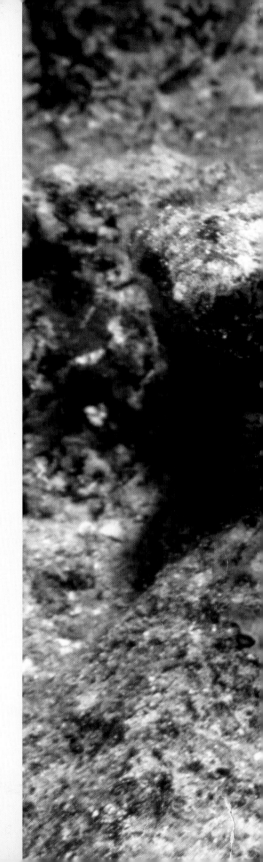

Sea stars have mouths
on their bottoms.
They eat while moving
along rocks and coral.

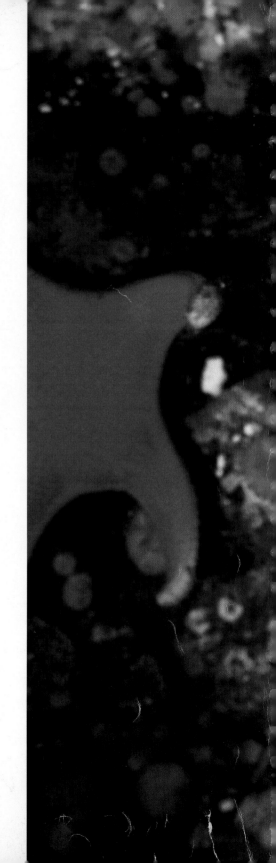

Awesome Bottoms

Soft or pointed,
smooth or smelly,
bottoms help animals
in many ways.

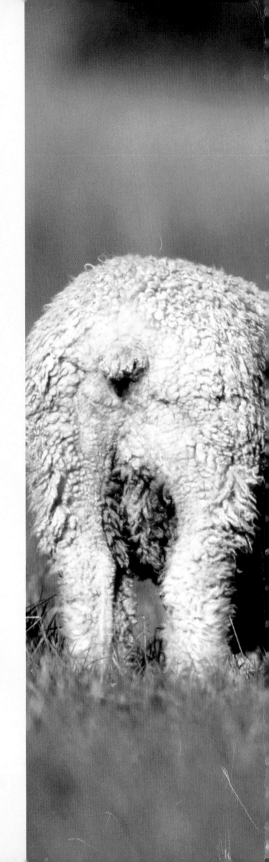

Glossary

coral—a substance found underwater that is made from the bodies of tiny sea animals

curious—to want to learn more about something

message—the information an animal gives through movement or other action

protect—to keep safe

Read More

Lynch, Wayne. *Whose Bottom Is This?* Name That Animal! Milwaukee: Gareth Stevens, 2003.

Manushkin, Fran. *The Tushy Book.* Orlando, Fla.: Harcourt, 2007.

Stephanides, Myrsini. *The Book of Baby Animal Butts.* Irvington, N.Y.: Hylas, 2006.

Internet Sites

FactHound offers a safe, fun way to find Internet sites related to this book. All of the sites on FactHound have been researched by our staff.

Here's how:

1. Visit *www.facthound.com*

2. Choose your grade level.

3. Type in this book ID **0736867155** for age-appropriate sites. You may also browse subjects by clicking on letters, or by clicking on pictures and words.

4. Click on the **Fetch It** button.

FactHound will fetch the best sites for you!

Index

Word Count: 131
Grade: 1
Early-Intervention Level: 15